Thomas the Tank Engine's

BIG YELLOW TREASURY

BY CHRISTOPHER AWDRY
ILLUSTRATIONS BY KEN STOTT

Random House · New York

Thomas

AND THE PONY SHOW

Thomas was waiting at the station. He saw
Becky and her mother come onto the platform.
They climbed on board, and off went Thomas.

Thomas knew Becky well. He often saw her riding her pony, Barnaby, as he puffed past the farm where she lived.

Sometimes Becky and Barnaby would be practicing jumping. Thomas was careful not to whistle in case he frightened the pony.

One day Thomas noticed workers in Fox's Field.
They were setting up for the Pony Show.

"I wish I could see the Pony Show," Thomas thought.
"Becky is sure to be there riding Barnaby."

Finally, the day of the show arrived. It was beautiful
and sunny. Thomas hummed happily as he ran
along the track.

But as he came around a curve, he saw
a horse trailer stopped by the side of the road.

Becky stood beside the horse trailer looking
worried. Her father was bending down next
to one of the front wheels.

"It looks as if they've broken down," said Thomas' driver. "Poor Becky. She will be disappointed if she has to miss the show."

When Thomas reached the next station, he saw the stationmaster and Sir Topham Hatt. A porter was waiting nearby.

While Thomas waited, the porter spoke to the guard.
Then Percy arrived pushing a special freight car.
Carefully they coupled it to Clarabel.

The guard went to tell Thomas' driver:
"Becky was on her way to the Pony Show with
Barnaby when her horse trailer broke down."

"Sir Topham Hatt has asked if Thomas will take Barnaby, Becky, and her mother to the show. Her father will wait for the repair truck."

The ticket collector shook his head when the pony was led onto the station platform. "Most unusual," he said as the porter opened the doors of the freight car.

Becky and her mother walked Barnaby up the ramp, and when the pony was safely shut in the stall, they sat down in the back. Thomas took off again.

Fox's Field was near the next station.
Quickly Becky led Barnaby off the train and
trotted him to the starting point.

Thomas was glad to see that Becky was smiling again. As she reached the starting point, her name was called out. She was just in time!

While Thomas watched, Barnaby jumped a clear round.
Everyone clapped and Thomas whistled excitedly:
"Peep pip pip peeeeeeep."

But Thomas had to go before the results were
announced. "I wonder if Becky will win a prize?"
he kept saying. "I do hope so."

The next day Becky and Barnaby were waiting for Thomas at the station. Barnaby was wearing a big red ribbon, and Becky had brought a yellow one for Thomas.

"Thank you, Thomas," she said happily.
"We would never have won without you."
Thomas was happy, too.

Thomas

GOES TO SCHOOL

Every day as Thomas puffed down his branch line,
he passed a village school.

As Thomas came around the curve in front of the school, he whistled, "Peep, peep! Hello! Here I am."

When the children in the playground heard Thomas, they stopped playing and ran to the wall to wave and smile.

"I'd like to go to school," said Thomas to Percy one day at the station.

"You're far too big to go to school," laughed
Sir Topham Hatt. "And far too useful!"

One afternoon when Thomas stopped by the school,
the children didn't wave or smile. A group of parents
and teachers were looking very serious.

Thomas saw a large banner hanging outside the school. His driver read it out loud: "Save our school from closing down! Come to our Grand Fair."

On the way home, Thomas' driver had an idea.
"I know," he said. "I can bring my two donkeys
to the fair to give rides to the children."

"And I've got a clown's costume at home," added
Thomas' fireman. "I'll come along and make the
children laugh."

That night in the engine shed, Thomas told Percy
and Toby about the school fair.

Thomas wanted to help, too. If the school closed down, he would miss seeing the children.

The morning of the fair arrived. Thomas' driver had to telephone Sir Topham Hatt with some bad news.

"Both my donkeys have a bad cough," said the driver.
"They can't come to the fair," he said.
"Don't worry," said Sir Topham Hatt. "I'll think of something."

Sir Topham Hatt thought for a while and then went to the shed. He told Thomas about the sick donkeys. "I want *you* to give the children rides instead."

Before long, Annie and Clarabel were decorated with balloons and Thomas was given a special polish.
Soon Thomas puffed into the siding next to the school.

The playground was already busy. Thomas' fireman, dressed as a clown, was making the children laugh. There were booths selling cupcakes and tea.

There were games to play and competitions to win.
But best of all, the children loved the rides on Thomas.

Thomas chugged happily up and down the track,
pulling Annie and Clarabel. Thomas was the main
attraction of the fair!

At the end of the day, Sir Topham Hatt counted
how much money they had raised.

"We have raised enough money today to save the school!" Sir Topham Hatt announced.
Everyone cheered.

Thomas was delighted that he had helped save the school. "Now you've been to school and been Really Useful, too!" laughed Sir Topham Hatt.

Henry

GOES TO THE HOSPITAL

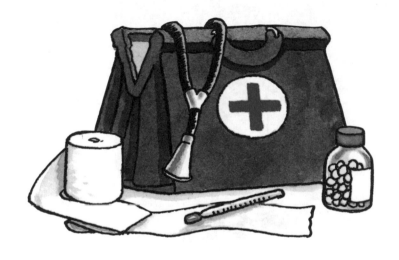

One morning when Henry was waiting at the station, he saw a nurse standing on the platform. "I'm going to work at the hospital," she told Henry's driver.

Every day Henry watched for the nurse. He liked her.
She always said "Hello" to him.
Then one morning the nurse wasn't there.

The ticket collector looked to see if she was coming,
but it was time to go, so the guard blew his whistle
and waved his green flag. The train left without her.

It was a stormy day and the rain fell as Henry
traveled slowly down the line. At the next station
the signal said STOP.

Henry's driver looked out of the cab to see what the
delay was. "There must be something wrong," he said.
"We've been held up here far too long."

Finally, the stationmaster arrived. "We need Henry's help," he said. "A little girl named Amy has hurt her leg and the ambulance is stuck in the mud."

"Can Henry take Amy to the station near the hospital?"
"Of course," said the driver.
Henry was delighted to help.

Soon two ambulance men appeared carrying Amy
on a stretcher, and there, walking by her side,
was the nurse.

"Don't worry, Amy," the nurse said, "Henry will soon get you safely to the hospital."

Gently the men placed the stretcher on the seat.
The nurse sat next to Amy and made sure that
she was comfortable.

When everything was ready, Henry set off. He traveled
very carefully so that Amy didn't hurt her leg again.

At the station near the hospital another ambulance met Amy and the nurse.

The ambulance men carried the stretcher past Henry, through a side gate, and out to the ambulance.

They took Amy to the hospital. There she saw
a doctor and had an X-ray of her leg taken.
The nurse showed Amy the picture.

Her ankle wasn't broken—only sprained.
"You're a lucky girl," said the nurse as she
bandaged Amy's ankle.

The nurse took Amy outside in a wheelchair.
"Can I go home on Henry's train?" she asked.

"You'll have to ask your mom," laughed the nurse. "Look, there she is."

Mom had brought the car to take Amy home,
but they went to the station first.

Henry was still at the station. Sir Topham Hatt had come to thank him, too. Henry felt very proud.

"Thank you for helping me," said Amy. "It was fun riding to the hospital on the train."

"You're a Really Useful Engine, Henry," said the nurse.
"Just like Thomas," said Henry happily.